Ink & Iron

A steamy small-town romance about a guarded veteran, a bold tattoo artist, and the ink that sparks something real.

Hana York

Pink Pop Publishing

Ink & Iron

(The Thorne Sisters Book 1)

Copyright © 2025 by Hana York

All rights reserved.

www.HanaYork.com

Contents

Prologue

LOLA

Mornings in Briar Hill smelled like coffee, motor oil, and gossip.

I propped the studio door open with a cinderblock I'd spray-painted black and gold, the edges still crusted with glitter from a Thorne sisters' DIY night gone sideways. It let in the breeze—and, sure enough, the scent of cinnamon rolls from Sweet Brew next door came drifting in like temptation wrapped in sugar.

Needle & Ink was quiet for now. Just the hum of my ancient tattoo machine warming up, the faint flicker of fluorescent light over the front desk, and the ghost of last night's playlist still echoing in the back of my head. This was my favorite time of day before the buzz. Before the pain and stories and secrets people etched into their skin like armor.

I wiped down my station for the third time. It didn't need it. I just needed to move.

Vivian texted twice already: Bring wine or don't bother showing up.

We had dinner plans at her place tonight—me, Eliza, Veronica, and Vivian. We were sisters by blood, bruises, or both. We didn't always agree, but we showed up, especially when Eliza cooked.

Vivian would bring the fire, Veronica the sarcasm. Eliza would bring heart-shaped napkins or something equally earnest.

And me? I'd show up with a bottle of red and pretend I wasn't the one who needed it the most.

The bell above the door jingled.

I looked up—and saw him.

Big. Broad. Shoulders like a wrecking ball. A jaw that had clenched its way through more than one war, if I had to guess. Dark eyes. Scar peeking from under the sleeve of a plain black tee.

He stepped inside like the world weighed too much.

And something in me leaned toward him before I could stop it.

Chapter One

TANNER

I almost turned around twice.

Once when I saw the sign—Needle & Ink scrawled across the glass in thick, stylized lettering like it dared you to walk through the door. And once when I saw her behind the counter.

She didn't look up at first. Just kept wiping down the same corner of her station with the kind of focus you only have when you're trying not to think too hard. Ink-stained fingers. Dark hair knotted on top of her head. Tank top. Tattoos up one arm and down the other.

She looked like every reason I shouldn't be here.

I stepped inside anyway.

The bell overhead jingled. She looked up. And for a second—just a beat too long—her eyes landed on me and stuck.

Something flickered across her face. Surprise. Curiosity. Heat?

Then she blinked, and it was gone. "You lost?" she asked, voice smooth, slightly amused. Like she already knew I wasn't the walk-in type.

I cleared my throat. "No. I was referred. A buddy of mine, Sam Bell. You did a piece for him a few months back."

Her eyes narrowed a little, but her mouth tugged into something that might've been a smile. "Forearm phoenix?"

I nodded.

She set the rag down, finally giving me her full attention—and that was a problem. Because now I couldn't stop looking. Or thinking about how long it had been since someone looked at me like that. Sharp. Like she was trying to figure out where I broke.

Her gaze dropped to my arm—the thick scar that curved down my arm and beneath my bicep, old and ugly, raised and pale against my skin.

She didn't flinch.

Didn't ask what happened.

Didn't pretend not to notice, either.

"I'm Tanner."

She nodded once. "Lola."

A beat passed between us—quiet, full of things neither of us said.

I cleared my throat. "Can you make it disappear?"

She stepped forward, slow and sure.

"No," she said. "But I can make it mean something else."

I should've left after that.

That would've been the smart move—turn around, say thanks but no thanks, and find a way to live with the thing carved into my skin.

But I didn't move.

I just stood there like some idiot who didn't know how to carry his own pain. Like I was waiting for her to tell me what to do with it.

Her eyes flicked back up to mine, steady and unreadable. "Do you have a design in mind?"

I shook my head. "No. Just know I don't want to see it anymore."

She nodded again as if that made perfect sense. "You want to book a consult or just talk now?"

Now. Before I lost the nerve.

"Now's fine."

She gestured toward her chair. "Sit."

It wasn't a request. It wasn't rude, either. Just... matter-of-fact. Like she already knew I'd listen.

I sat.

The chair hissed under my weight, the leather cracked and worn from use. The studio smelled like antiseptic, old ink, and something warm and clean, like citrus and cedar. Her, maybe.

She moved quietly around me, grabbing a sketchpad and pencil. Every motion efficient, precise. No small talk. No pity. Just focus.

I tried not to stare. I failed.

There was something about her—some mix of stillness and heat that didn't make sense.

"I won't ask what happened," she said without looking up, pencil moving fast over the page. "But if you want the design to mean something, I need to know what kind of story you're trying to rewrite."

Her voice was quiet. Nonthreatening.

Still hit like a sucker punch.

I didn't answer.

But I didn't get up, either.

LOLA

He didn't talk.

That didn't surprise me.

What surprised me was that he stayed.

Most guys with that kind of scar—military bearing, thousand-yard stare, whole body held like it's bracing for an impact that already happened—they don't sit. They ghost. They cancel. They postpone.

But not this one. Tanner.

He sat down like he didn't know why he was doing it, just that something told him he should.

And God help me, I noticed everything.

Not just the scar. The *man*.

The way he moved—deliberate and stiff, like his body wasn't entirely his. The cut of his jaw under that scruff. The thick forearms that flexed when he crossed them like he was holding himself in place. The long, quiet breath he took when he looked around my studio.

And yeah, fine, he was hot in that *haunted, ex-soldier, too-broad-for-this-chair* kind of way. But it wasn't just that. It was the way he looked at me, like he wasn't used to being seen. Not like that. Not like a person.

I knew that feeling.

I picked up a pencil and gave my hands something to do before they did something reckless. Like touch him.

"I won't ask what happened," I said, eyes on the sketch-pad. "But if you want the design to mean something, I need to know what kind of story you're trying to rewrite."

He didn't answer. Didn't leave, either. That was something.

I kept sketching—lines, shapes, movement. Nothing permanent yet. Just breathing space between us.

But my pulse had already picked up. And it wasn't just professional curiosity.

This man was carrying a war inside him.

And for the first time in a long time, I wanted to help someone put themselves back together.

Even if it meant breaking my own rules.

I didn't usually let clients rattle me.

They came in with their heartbreak, their grief, their declarations of rebellion. I gave them ink and shape and permanence. That was the deal. I didn't carry it. I translated it.

But Tanner sat in my chair like he didn't know how to stop hurting.

And I hated how much I wanted to be the one to stop the hurt.

He didn't fidget. Didn't scroll his phone. Didn't fill the silence with nervous chatter like most people did when they were afraid to be alone with themselves.

He just... watched.

I liked that he didn't pretend. Didn't fake ease or flirt. He was just raw and quiet and *there*. And the air between us felt like it was holding its breath.

I added a curve to the shoulder of the design, something that would trace the edge of the scar without trying to erase it. I could feel his gaze on my hands—not in a creepy way, but just... aware. Present.

"What kind of thing are you thinking?" he asked finally, voice low and rough. Like he hadn't used it in a while.

I glanced up, our eyes meeting for half a second too long.

"Something that fits," I said, my voice steady despite my stomach having other ideas. "Not something that hides."

He nodded once. Said nothing else.

But he didn't look away, either.

And I couldn't decide if I wanted to draw faster just to get him out of here—or slower, so he'd stay.

Chapter Two

TANNER

S he didn't rush.

That was the first thing I noticed.

Most people get uncomfortable in silence. They talk. Fill it with noise or bullshit or questions they don't really want answered.

But Lola just... let it be quiet. Let me breathe.

And still, somehow, I couldn't.

I watched her work, the way her fingers moved—steady, confident, stained with ink. There was a softness under the edge like she'd built armor around something breakable and dared the world to try her.

And God, I shouldn't have been thinking about her fingers.

Or her mouth.

Or the curve of her back as she leaned over the sketch-pad.

I wasn't here for that.

I was here because I hadn't slept through the night in months. Because every time I looked at that scar, I saw the moment I didn't save him. And because some idiot friend of mine said she was good at turning shit into art.

He didn't mention she looked like that.

Didn't say I'd feel something just being in the same room.

I didn't like it.

Didn't like how I wanted her to keep talking, even though every word scraped at nerves I thought I'd buried.

"What kind of thing are you thinking?" I asked because I needed to say something, anything before I did something even dumber—like ask if I could see her tattoos up close.

She looked up. And Jesus.

It was just a glance. A flick of dark eyes, sharp and knowing. But it hit like a punch to the ribs.

"Something that fits," she said. "Not something that hides."

I swallowed. Nodded. Said nothing.

But I didn't move.

I wouldn't. Not until she put something over that scar. Maybe not even after.

She angled the sketchpad toward me. Not a complete design—just the bones. Shape. Flow.

A tree. Twisted. Weathered. But still standing.

Branches reaching upward. Roots sinking deep. One half inked in heavy black lines, the other lighter, almost like it had been sketched and half erased.

"It's just an idea," she said, watching my face. "I can change it. Or scrap it entirely."

I stared at it longer than I meant to.

It shouldn't have hit me like that.

But it did.

"It's..." I cleared my throat. "Yeah."

Yeah.

That was all I could give her.

Because *saying* what it meant—admitting what it reminded me of, what that scar stood for—would've cracked something I wasn't ready to face in front of a woman who looked at me like she already saw too much.

"You sure?" she asked, voice gentler this time.

"No," I said honestly. "But I think it's the first thing that hasn't made me want to walk out of a room in a while."

She didn't smile. But something softened in her eyes.

"Alright," she said, tearing the sheet off and setting it aside. "I'll refine the lines and pull together some options. Come back tomorrow, and we'll get started."

I nodded and stood.

She moved closer to grab something off the counter, and for a second, we were side by side—close enough that I could smell the citrus in her shampoo and feel the warmth radiating off her skin.

She didn't look at me.

I didn't look at her.

But it felt like we both noticed.

"Same time?" I asked, already at the door.

She didn't turn around.

"Same time."

LOLA

Vivian opened the door in stilettos and a silk robe as if she wasn't hosting three sisters and a bubbling lasagna.

It was Vivian's apartment, but Eliza had taken over the kitchen—because Vivian didn't cook. Takeout was her art form. The only reason her oven had seen anything more ambitious than reheated Pad Thai was because Eliza treat-ed it like her own.

"Wine?" she asked, already walking away.

I held up the bottle I brought. "Way ahead of you."

Veronica was camped out on the couch, legs tucked un-der her, sipping red and pretending she wasn't critiquing the entire room's energy. Eliza popped out of the kitchen wearing an apron with dancing eggplants.

"Dinner's almost ready!" she said with the kind of sunny cheer that made me want to check for hidden Xanax.

I handed her the wine, dropped onto the nearest chair, and kicked off my boots. "You know, normal people eat in clothes they can stain."

Vivian flicked a hand. "Normal people are boring. And I'm not the one wielding marinara."

Veronica arched a brow. "That's true love. Silk robe near red sauce? Risky."

Vivian winked. "I like to live dangerously."

We all laughed, and for a moment, the room felt easy—like the years of damage, drama, and tangled fa-ther-based trauma didn't hang between us like old smoke.

Then Eliza set down a bowl of garlic knots and turned her too-bright smile on me.

"So," she said. "Anything new at the shop?"

I stabbed a knot with my fork. "A guy came in today."

Three sets of eyebrows lifted in unison.

Veronica leaned forward. "Tattoo client or tall, dark, broody mistake?"

I shrugged, keeping my face neutral. "Tattoo client. Big. Quiet. Ex-military, I think."

Vivian's eyes gleamed. "Oooh. The strong-silent-'will-definitely-ruin-you-in-bed' type?"

"Viv," Eliza scolded, cheeks pink.

I didn't answer.

Which was probably answer enough.

We finished off two bottles of wine, the pan of lasagna, and half a tiramisu Eliza insisted was "experimental," which meant she'd tried a new recipe and immediately regretted it.

Vivian kicked us out around nine with a dramatic yawn and a vague threat about needing her beauty sleep. Veronica stayed behind—ostensibly to help clean up, but probably just to snoop through Vivian's beauty products.

They were twins—Vivian and Veronica. Identical in face, but that's where the similarities ended. Vivian was all fire and flair, born to be onstage. Veronica didn't need volume—she could silence a room with one eyebrow and a better vocabulary. Calm, composed, and secretly the most dangerous of all of us.

Eliza hugged me a little too tightly at the door. "You okay?"

"Course," I said. "Just full of wine and sibling judgment."

She didn't buy it, but she let me go.

***

When I got home, my apartment above the shop was quiet. It still smelled faintly of ink and lemon oil. I kicked off my boots, stripped to a tank and shorts, and sat on the edge of my bed without turning the lights on.

I didn't usually bring clients home in my head. I left them at the shop with the needles, ink, and stories they didn't want to carry alone.

But Tanner had followed me here.

The way he sat so still. Like he didn't trust his body anymore. The way he looked at me—guarded, wary, but watching. Like he needed something and hated that he did.

Like I was a risk he hadn't decided to take.

And damn it, he'd gotten under my skin faster than any man had in a long time.

I wasn't thinking about his scar.

I was thinking about his mouth. His hands. The weight of him in that chair and how my pulse had spiked every time he leaned forward.

He was coming back tomorrow.

I should've been focused on the design. The lines. The meaning.

Instead, I lay back on the bed, stared at the ceiling, and whispered to the dark:

"Don't be stupid, Lola."

Chapter Three

LOLA

The shop was too quiet.

Which was ridiculous because I liked it quiet in the mornings. The hum of the machines. The scent of antiseptic and eucalyptus cleaner. The creak of the old floorboards beneath my boots. Usually, it settled me.

Today, it didn't.

I'd already rearranged my ink trays twice, restocked the disposable razors, and changed the liner in the sharps container—none of which were urgent, and all of which I was doing just to keep my hands busy.

Because he was coming back.

I hadn't even touched him yet—hadn't so much as wiped down the scar—but he was already under my skin.

I didn't know what I expected. Maybe that he'd ghost. That he'd let whatever pulled him in yesterday get swallowed by whatever made him bolt in the first place.

But he'd booked the appointment. Said he'd be back.

And it was almost time.

I rechecked the clock like that would make him materialize.

The bell over the door jingled.

I didn't flinch.

But my pulse sure as hell did.

He stepped inside, still all shadows and silence. Same black T-shirt, different jeans. Hair damp like he'd just showered. Clean-shaven. Or clean-ish. The scruff had a purpose now.

And the minute our eyes met, I knew I was screwed.

Because it wasn't just attraction. It was something more profound. Like recognition. Like my bones already knew him.

"Morning," I said, nodding toward him.

"Let's do it," he said.

And just like that, I forgot what peace had ever felt like.

I nodded toward the back room. "We'll work in the private suite. Better lighting."

And fewer eyes. Not that there were any this early, but I didn't need the front windows catching me staring at this man like I hadn't seen muscles before.

He followed without a word, boots solid against the wood. I could feel him behind me, heavy presence, silent intensity. It did things to me I didn't have names for.

Inside, I gestured to the chair. "Shirt off."

He hesitated—not out of modesty. No, this was something else. A breath. A brace. Like shedding a layer wasn't just fabric—it was armor.

But then he did it.

And I had to focus on keeping my professional face when all I wanted to do was stare.

The scar was even more brutal under the fluorescent lights. It was pale and raised, jagged in places, old but angry, and surrounded by muscle that was very much not angry—just... distracting.

I pulled on gloves. "I'm going to clean the area first. Let me know if anything's uncomfortable."

"Already is," he muttered, but there wasn't bite in it.

I stepped closer, cotton pad in hand, antiseptic in the other. Pressed gently to his skin. He didn't move or flinch, but his jaw flexed just once, sharp and silent.

I told myself I was studying the canvas, mapping the lines, and focusing on how the ink would wrap around the damage.

But my hand lingered. Just a beat too long.

"You tense like you expect it to hurt," I said, soft.

"Doesn't?"

"Not yet."

He glanced down, eyes catching mine. "You always get this close?"

I lifted a brow. "Only when I'm working."

And then I turned back to the tray because if I didn't, I would have done something really unprofessional.

Like find out how that tension tasted.

TANNER

I'd taken a hit to the ribs on a mission once. Cracked clean through. Breathing felt like fire for weeks.

This?

This was worse.

Not because it hurt—but because it didn't.

Her hands were steady. Gloved. Clinical. But I felt it straight through the bone every time she touched me.

Her hands moved over the scar like it didn't intimidate her.

Like she wasn't afraid of what it meant or what it might still hold.

Most people either stared too long or pretended not to see it. She did neither. She just worked with a calm that made it hard to breathe.

She was standing close enough that I could smell her shampoo again—citrus and something clean. No perfume. No drama. Just her. Simple. Real.

I couldn't remember the last time someone touched me without flinching first. Without a clipboard in hand. Without checking for wounds or measuring damage. Just touch—warm and unguarded.

"You tense like you expect it to hurt," she said quietly.

"Doesn't?"

"Not yet."

I looked down, caught her eyes, and regretted it instantly. Not because of what I saw—but because of what I felt. Like if I stayed in that moment too long, I'd unravel.

"You always get this close?" I asked, mostly because I needed something to say before I said something *stupid*.

She didn't blink. Just lifted one perfect brow. "Only when I'm working."

Then she turned away, and I was grateful—and disappointed.

Jesus. What the hell was wrong with me?

I should've been focused on the design. The lines. The damn scar.

Instead, I was thinking about her mouth.

About how she hadn't asked for my story but already felt like she knew it.

About how I wasn't sure I'd want to leave when this was over.

Which was the one thing I absolutely shouldn't want.

She returned with the stencil in one hand and a quiet focus in her eyes. The kind that said she'd already seen everything she needed to, even if I hadn't said a word.

"You good with black and grey?" she asked, voice back to business.

"Yeah. Color doesn't feel right."

"Didn't think it would."

She pressed the stencil gently to my skin, smoothing it over the scar with practiced fingers. I knew I was supposed to be paying attention to placement, but instead, I was counting her heartbeats by the rhythm in her touch.

"You always this quiet?" she asked, not looking at me.

"Depends."

"On what?"

"If I've got something to say."

That earned me a glance. Just a flicker of a smirk at the corner of her mouth.

"And here I thought you were brooding for the aesthetic."

"Do I look like a man who cares about aesthetics?"

Her gaze dropped to the stencil she'd just set, then back to me. "You came to a tattoo artist to cover a scar. So yeah. I'd say there's a little vanity in there."

That made me laugh—short, low, and unexpected.

She looked almost smug about it.

"What about you?" I asked. "You always this direct?"

"Only when I'm awake."

I shook my head, still smiling.

She wiped the stencil with a clean cloth, careful, focused. "You from around here?"

"No. Just passing through. A friend who lives nearby said I should come to see you."

"Right. Sam Bell."

"Yeah. He said you were good."

"Didn't say I was charming?"

I looked at her then—really looked.

"Figured that out on my own."

Chapter Four

LOLA

I 'd been called many things—hot, intense, intimidating. "Charming" wasn't usually on the list. Not that I needed it to be.

I was joking when I said it.

But then he looked at me—quiet, steady, all heat and honesty—and said, *"Figured that out on my own."*

It wasn't a flirt. It wasn't even a line.

It was just true.

I covered it with a smirk. "Careful. You keep saying nice things; I might start to think you like me."

He didn't blink. "Would that be a problem?"

God.

His tone wasn't cocky. It wasn't defensive. It was just... honest. Steady. Like if he said it, he meant it. No armor. No pretense. Just him.

I cleared my throat and turned back to the machine. "Alright, let's get this going. Sit back and try not to flex. Not that I'm judging—it just makes my job harder when guys try to impress me mid-line."

"I'll try to behave," he said, and that damn voice of his did something warm and wrong to my insides.

I snapped on a fresh pair of gloves and rolled my stool closer. "This part might sting."

"I've had worse."

"Bet you have."

And then I pressed the machine to his skin, and the room went quiet except for the hum of the needle—and the space between us that felt anything but still.

The machine hummed steadily in my hand, low and familiar. Tanner didn't even blink when I hit the first stretch of scar tissue. Most guys twitched. Flinched. Tried to play it cool.

He just stayed still. Silent. Like he was used to pain showing up and sticking around.

"Guess I should've warned you—I talk when I work," I said lightly. "Occupational hazard."

"Yeah?"

"Yeah. Helps keep people from passing out. Or panicking. Or making me listen to their breakup playlists."

A hint of a smile tugged at the corner of his mouth. "No panic here."

"Mm. Strong silent type. Knew it."

I leaned in, focusing on the curve of the design. "I've got three sisters. We could fill a room with noise and still not get a word in edgewise."

He glanced at me. Not much, but enough.

"I'm guessing you didn't grow up with that kind of chaos," I said.

"No."

That was it. One syllable. But it didn't feel like a wall, more like a line drawn in the dirt, waiting to see if I'd cross it.

"Veronica owns a sex shop, Vivian runs a burlesque club, and Eliza teaches kindergarten. So, depending on who you ask, we're either empowering women, corrupting society, or overachieving in the baked goods department."

His brow lifted slightly. "And you?"

"I make art out of pain," I said, pressing gently over the ink. "You be the judge."

He was quiet for a second.

"Then I'm starting to think I came to the right place."

My hand didn't shake, but it was a near thing.

I didn't look up. Just kept the machine moving like my pulse hadn't just done something complicated.

TANNER

Lola talked while she worked. Just like she said she would.

Stories about past clients, all of them ridiculous. A guy who passed out and woke up flirting. A woman who cried because her tiny finger-heart wasn't "emotional enough."

The one that stuck with me was a bachelorette party that came in for matching peaches. One of them passed out halfway through and still swears hers is crooked.

"It's not," Lola had said. "Her left butt cheek just flexes weird when she laughs."

She'd said it with a straight face like it was just another Tuesday.

It should've been noise. A distraction.

But it worked.

Her voice kept me tethered—kept me from getting pulled under by the sound of the needle and the weight of everything behind it.

I didn't mean to say anything.

But somewhere between a story about a guy who wanted a skull made out of kittens and how her fingers shifted over the curve of my arm, it just... slipped out.

"I almost didn't come in."

She didn't miss a beat. "Why?"

I kept my eyes forward. "Because the last time I tried to cover it, I made it as far as the stencil before I walked out."

She didn't say anything.

Just let me keep going.

"I got the scar the day I lost someone. A brother in every way but blood. I carried him out, but it wasn't enough. Hasn't felt like enough since."

Her machine didn't slow. Her hands didn't hesitate.

But her voice went quieter. "You're not the first person to walk in here trying to make peace with something like that."

I finally looked at her.

"Maybe not, but you're the first person who made me think that might actually be possible."

She looked up.

I saw the truth in her eyes.

Then she said, "Not everything painful needs to be erased. Some things deserve to become something new."

She didn't say anything else. Just turned back to the piece and finished the last few lines with a kind of focus that didn't feel clinical anymore.

It felt personal.

When she finally pulled the machine away and peeled off her gloves, the hum in the room faded, but something else lingered. Something quieter. Heavier.

"That's it for today," she said, voice low. "We'll let it settle and finish the shading tomorrow."

I nodded, even though I wasn't ready to move. My arm felt warm and raw but steady. Like something had shifted under the skin—and not just the ink.

She reached for the bandage and paused like she was about to say something else. Then didn't. Just wrapped the area with practiced care, her fingers brushing the inside of my wrist.

She didn't ask if I was okay.

Didn't tell me I'd be fine.

She just looked up and said, "Same time?"

"Yeah," I said. "I'll be here."

I pulled my shirt back on, rolled my shoulder, and reached the door before turning back.

"You don't talk just to fill silence," I said.

Her brow lifted.

"You talk so people don't disappear into it."

She held my gaze and gave a single, deliberate nod.

Nothing more—but it was enough.

Chapter Five

LOLA

I was in trouble.

Deep, dangerous, "don't say I didn't warn you" kind of trouble.

Not that I'd admit it. Not even to my sisters. Especially not to my sisters.

He came back.

Honest, intense, makes-me-want-to-break-my-own-rules Tanner. And I was doing an even worse job of keeping him out of my head than yesterday.

"Same time?" I'd asked, trying not to sound eager.

"Yeah," he said. "I'll be here."

And damn it, I couldn't stop thinking about the way he said it—like he'd already decided this meant something.

I should've been thrilled. This was what I did. What I loved. People brought me their scars—physical and otherwise—and let me help them turn pain into art. But Tanner wasn't just another client, and we both knew it.

The smart thing would've been to keep my distance. To focus on the design and pretend like hell he wasn't getting under my skin so fast it might as well have been permanent ink.

Instead, here I was, watching the clock and feeling like a teenager waiting for her first crush to call.

Get it together, Lola.

I had two hours before he showed up again, which was plenty of time to pull myself together and remember how to be a professional.

Instead, I spent those two hours picking up the phone twice before finally calling Veronica.

"Pleasure & Co.," she answered. "How can I—"

"Hey, it's me."

"Ugh, you ruined my customer service voice. What's up?"

"You free?"

"I can be. Vivian said you were acting weird at dinner last night."

I rolled my eyes even though she couldn't see it. "Thanks, spy twins."

"So? Was she right?"

I sighed. "Meet me at Sweet Brew in ten?"

"Ten it is."

She hung up before I could change my mind.

Veronica was already at a table when I got there, drinking what looked like half coffee, half cream. She arched a brow as I slid into the seat across from her.

"You seem surprisingly on edge for a woman who got laid last night."

"I didn't," I said, stealing a sip of her drink.

"Didn't get laid? Or didn't do anything to make you this twitchy?"

"Both."

"Huh." She watched me over the rim of her mug. "Then why do you look like you've been staring at your phone all morning, waiting for a guy to text?"

"Because he's coming back, and I can't get him out of my head," I said, hating how it sounded. "I need you to talk some sense into me."

Veronica's lips curved into a slow, knowing smile. "Tell me everything."

I filled her in—Tanner walking in like a storm cloud, his honesty, his silence, the way he made my pulse forget every rule I'd set for myself.

When I finally shut up long enough to breathe, Veronica just shook her head. "You're screwed."

"Gee that's comforting."

"You want comfort? Talk to Eliza." She leaned closer. "You want the truth? You're fighting a losing battle and loving every second of it."

"I don't love anything about this," I said, but my voice lacked conviction.

She gave me a look that said she wasn't buying it. "Lola, you've been walking around with an emotional chastity belt ever since—"

"Don't."

"Fine. Since your last 'adventure.' But this guy? He sounds different. You said it yourself—he's not just another client."

She was right, and it killed me.

I'd let one man get too close before. Watched him walk away because I wouldn't let my walls come down fast enough for him.

"I don't do this, Vee."

"Maybe you should," she said, tone gentle but unyielding.

I didn't answer.

TANNER

When I needed to clear my head, I ran.

Always had. Miles of nothing but breath and blood and grit between me and the things I didn't want to think about.

Today, it didn't work.

I pounded down the side streets around my place, gravel crunching under my sneakers, lungs burning — but every time I thought I could outrun it, there she was.

Lola.

Sharp smile. Quick hands. Those wild, steady eyes that made me feel like maybe I wasn't broken past fixing after all.

I slowed to a walk, dragging a hand over my face, breath misting in the early morning air.

Goddamn it.

This wasn't supposed to happen.A tattoo. A cover-up. That was it.Not...whatever the hell was happening now.

I pulled out my phone without thinking, scrolling to Sam Bell's name. The guy who sent me to Needles & Ink in the first place. The guy who, apparently, had been holding out.

He picked up on the second ring. "Bell."

"It's me," I said, still catching my breath. "You got a second?"

"For you? Always. What's up?"

"You could've warned me."

There was a beat of silence. Then, a knowing laugh. "Let me guess. You met Lola."

"Yeah." I kicked a rock off the path, watching it skitter into the gutter. "She's...fire."

"Told you she was the best."

"That's not what I meant," I muttered.

Another laugh. "Buddy, if I'd told you the truth, you would've chickened out."

"Maybe," I admitted. "Or maybe I just would've prepared better."

There was a pause, longer this time.

"You good?" Sam asked, tone shifting.

I stared down the empty street, the pulse in my chest not all from the run anymore. "Yeah. Just...wasn't expecting this."

"What, feeling something that doesn't suck?"

I huffed out a laugh despite myself. "Something like that."

Sam's voice softened. "Look, man. You've been carrying that weight for a long time. You deserve something good. Don't fuck it up by overthinking it."

"Wasn't planning to."

"Good." Another pause. "She's one of the good ones, Tanner. Careful with her."

I nodded, even though he couldn't see me. "I know."

We hung up, and I stood there for a long minute, feeling the weight of the conversation settle in my chest.

Careful with her.

Yeah.

But something told me I wasn't the only one who needed someone to be careful.

I jogged the last few blocks back to my place, showered fast, changed, and sat on the edge of my bed, lacing up my boots.

Same time, she'd said.

I'd be there.

And this time, I wasn't just showing up for the ink.

I was showing up for her.

For whatever this was.For whatever it could be.

No walls. No halfway.Not this time.

Chapter Six

LOLA

I wasn't great at sitting still. Never had been.

But after meeting Veronica for coffee and getting a pep talk disguised as a verbal smackdown, I found myself back at the shop, staring at the clock like a lovesick idiot.

Tanner wouldn't be here for another hour.

I grabbed my sketchpad, flipping past a few half-finished designs, and started to draw. Something simple. Clean lines. Maybe a floral wrap or a geometric pattern. Something that didn't make me think about broad shoulders, quiet, steady hands, or a mouth that could ruin a girl with a single look.

I was halfway through a rough design when I realized I'd started sketching a pair of sharp, clear, intense eyes.

Tanner's eyes.

I muttered a curse under my breath and flipped the page, trying to shake him out of my head.

The phone buzzed across the table.

I grabbed it without thinking, half-hoping it was him. Instead: Eliza.

I smiled, even as a tiny knot of worry formed in my gut. Eliza didn't call in the middle of a workday unless something was wrong.

I answered immediately. "Hey, sunshine. Who do I need to take out?"

There was a sniff on the other end of the line. "No one. I'm fine."

Liar.

I straightened in my chair, all pretense of sketching forgotten. "Talk to me, Eliza."

She let out a shaky breath. "It's stupid."

"It's never stupid if it's making you feel like this."

Another breath. "One of the moms at school. She... she said I was too young to understand real responsibility. That being 'cute' isn't the same as being capable."

I felt my blood pressure spike immediately.

"Eliza—" I started, already planning a full-scale take-down.

"I know," she said quickly. "I know it doesn't matter. I know it's just one person's opinion. But it got under my skin, you know?"

Yeah. I knew.

People saw what they wanted to see, especially with someone like Eliza—bright, sweet, open Eliza—who wore her heart on her sleeve and didn't realize how fragile it could sometimes be.

I leaned back in the chair, pressing a hand over my eyes.

"You are responsible as hell, and you're more capable than half the jackasses walking around this town," I said fiercely. "That woman's just jealous because you've got a heart and a brain, and she's got a minivan and a superiority complex."

Eliza let out a watery laugh.

I smiled, but it twisted a little in my chest.

Because for all the teasing and chaos between us, Eliza was *ours*.

Technically, she had a different mom—the one Dad left ours for. But it had never mattered—not once. She was our sister in every way that counted; anyone who made her feel like she was less could catch hands.

"You're good, Eliza," I said, voice low. "Better than most people deserve. Don't let one bitter woman make you forget that."

There was a soft sniff. "Thanks, Lola."

"Anytime. You want me to come down there and glare at her until she cries?"

She laughed, a little stronger this time. "Maybe later."

"Good. Because I have a client coming in soon, and I need to pretend I'm a respectable business owner for at least another hour."

"You are a respectable business owner."

I grinned. "Don't tell anyone. I've got a reputation to maintain."

We hung up a few minutes later, and I set the phone down, staring at the wall.

It was funny, the lines we drew around ourselves. The walls we built. We thought they kept us safe.

But sometimes they just kept the wrong people out.

The bell over the door jingled, and I looked up.

Tanner stepped inside—solid and steady, like he belonged there—and smiled at me in a way that made my heart do something reckless and stupid.

Yeah.

Maybe it was time to stop hiding behind the walls.

Maybe it was time to see what could happen if I let someone in.

Really let them in.

TANNER

I wasn't restless. Not anymore. The run had burned off the worst of it—the sharp edges, the confusion, the instinct to bolt when something felt too real.

But it hadn't burned out the part of me that wanted her.

That part felt stronger than ever.

So instead of pacing circles around my life like I usually did when shit got complicated, I found myself pulling open the door to Needle & Ink like it wasn't even a decision anymore.

Like it was inevitable.

She looked up when I stepped inside—and damn.

One look at her, sitting there like a storm I wanted to walk into, and every excuse I'd ever used to keep people at arm's length went up in smoke.

The music was different today. It had a slow bass line and a steady drum. It matched the beat in my chest—all anticipation, hunger, and need.

"Right on time," she said, voice smooth as the track spinning through the speakers.

"Hope you haven't been staring at the clock."

"Don't flatter yourself," she said, but a spark in her eyes made me think maybe she had. At least once.

Then she smiled, small but real, and it knocked the breath out of me all over again.

"You ready?" she asked, nodding toward the back room.

Was I? Hell no. But that didn't stop me from following her.

I wasn't ready. Not for the way she'd slipped under my skin without a needle. And definitely not for the way I wanted more of whatever this was—more of her. She hadn't turned on the overhead lights, just a warm lamp in the corner that gave the room a quieter, more intimate feel. The kind of light that didn't hide anything but didn't blast it into view, either.

"Shirt off," she said, already snapping on gloves.

I hesitated again. Not because I minded stripping down—but because every time I did, it felt like letting her see more than I knew how to cover. But then I did it. And I saw something in her eyes that made it worth the risk. It wasn't pity. It wasn't shock, sympathy, or any other reactions I hated. It was understanding. Like she knew what else came off with that shirt—and liked me better for it.

She rolled closer, machine in hand. "You look tense."

"Been that way a while," I said.

"Doesn't have to stay that way." She smiled—full this time, bright and unguarded—and it did more damage than any needle. Made me want to lean in, like a moth to a flame with no sense of self-preservation.

I just shook my head and watched her work.

She hit the first line and didn't bother with distraction. Didn't talk. Just focused on the design taking shape on my arm, on the scar. Like she knew, the only thing that kept me here was her—her hands, her eyes, her silence.

"Thought you said you talk when you work," I said finally, missing the sound of her voice.

She scooted closer, gaze never leaving the ink. "Only when people need it."

Her knee brushed mine. Not an accident. Not an apology. Just contact. And that was almost worse than anything she could've said.

"You think I don't?" I asked quietly.

She didn't answer right away.

Didn't look up.

But when she spoke, her voice was soft and sure. "I think you're stronger than you let yourself believe."

And there it was—that feeling again. Like she saw through every defense I'd ever put up and knew exactly who I was underneath.

"Guess that makes one of us," I said finally.

The needle kept going, but her hands were gentle. Careful. Like she knew she was leaving more than ink behind.

We didn't talk after that. Didn't need to. There was something better than words between us—something real and raw, like the lines weaving their way across my skin. It felt different this time. Less like covering a wound and more like letting it breathe.

When she finished, she peeled off her gloves and drew back just enough for air to find its way between us again. But not enough for me to feel like it had really returned.

"Same time tomorrow?" she asked, pulling the bandage tight.

I nodded. "You know it."

"See you, Tanner."

I went to the door without looking back. If I had, if I'd seen the way she watched me go, I might've stayed. Given in to whatever the hell this was pulling so tight between us. But I made it outside—back into the daylight and air that didn't smell like her—before letting out a breath I didn't know I'd been holding.

And that's when I saw the sky.

Going dark, low, and sudden. The kind of storm that hit fast and hard, unexpected as a sniper round.

I cursed under my breath and headed for my truck in long, deliberate strides.

I'd make it out ahead of the worst of it.

Get back to the rental. Let my head clear.

Maybe even convince myself this thing with Lola—this reckless want that felt more dangerous than anything else—wasn't going to happen.

But then my damn truck wouldn't start.

I sat in the driver's seat for longer than I should've, fingers flexing on the steering wheel like they could squeeze life back into an engine that wouldn't turned over.

Raindrops pelted against the windshield.

Harder. Louder.

A crack of thunder split the air, too close to ignore.

I didn't want to walk back in there. Didn't want her to see me stranded or helpless. But the storm had other plans.

With a half-sighed curse, I got out and headed back inside.

Chapter Seven

LOLA

I was cleaning up, trying not to think about how his voice sounded when he said, "You know it," when the bell over the door jingled again.

He stepped inside, wet around the edges and looking like a storm just tried to kill him.

For a second, I thought he'd changed his mind. That he was coming back to finish what we'd barely started letting ourselves want. But then I saw the set of his shoulders, how his jaw flexed once and held.

"Truck's dead," he said, shaking rain from his hair. "Mind if I wait out the worst of it?"

I didn't flinch, but my pulse did. "Sure. No problem."

His eyes met mine—dark, searching. Like he hadn't expected me to say yes.

"Really," I said. "It's fine." Then, because I couldn't help myself: "You look like you could use a drink."

He hesitated again, like accepting anything more would be more complicated than just sitting through a storm.

But then he nodded. "Wouldn't say no."

I went to the back and grabbed a couple of beers from the mini fridge, heart thudding in my chest like it knew exactly how close I was to trouble.

"Not fancy," I said, extending one as I came out.

He took it and followed me to the back of the shop where I kept a beat-up leather couch for clients who needed more time than I could give them in the chair.

"Didn't peg you for a beer drinker," he said, settling in at the other end.

"First mistake," I said, cracking mine open and trying not to look like I was cataloging every single way he'd gotten under my skin.

Another crack of thunder split the sky, shaking the windows.

"You weren't kidding about it getting worse," he said, glancing outside.

"No," I said. "This might be the kind of storm that hangs around for a while."

A pause. A single breath suspended between us.

"Guess I'm not going anywhere soon," he said, voice low.

I should've nodded. Laughed it off. Said something that shut this down before we got in any deeper than we already were.

Instead, I took a long pull from my beer and smiled like I knew exactly how much trouble I was courting. "Guess not."

We sat silently for a few minutes, the rain pounding harder now—insistent, unrelenting. Like it was determined to soak everything in its path.

"You got a lot of these?" he asked, gesturing to the walls where sketches were pinned like memories.

"A few." I shrugged. "I get bored easily."

Something flickered across his face—a mix of surprise and curiosity.

"What?" I asked, taking a sip.

"Never met anyone like you," he said.

And there it was again. The honesty hit like a gut punch. I should've deflected. Should've said something sarcastic.

Instead, I heard myself say, "Good."

I didn't usually do this—didn't let clients linger or let myself care what they said when—but Tanner was different. He made me want things I wasn't supposed to want. He made me feel reckless.

And God help me. I liked it more than I should've.

Something low and rough moved through his throat. Almost a laugh. Almost a sound he didn't let himself make. I felt it under my skin, even if he didn't let it out.

"You don't pull punches, do you?" he asked.

I shook my head. "Not my style."

"Yeah," he said, a fire lighting behind those dark eyes. "I can see that."

And then we just sat there, beer in hand, listening to the storm rumble and boom like it had something to prove. There was too much space between us and not enough at the same time. My pulse was doing things I couldn't control.

He took a long drink and tipped his head back against the couch, eyes closed for half a second before he looked at me again.

"You ever done this before?" he asked.

"What?"

"Let someone hang around like this."

"No," I said honestly.

It didn't faze him. He didn't ask why I was letting him now—maybe because he already knew the answer or perhaps because it was easier not to say it out loud. I should've been trying to hide how much I wanted him there, but instead, I wondered what would happen if I let myself want more.

I watched him from under my lashes, heart racing. He looked good there—too damn good. Like he belonged on that old leather couch more than any client ever had. Like maybe I'd been waiting for him to show up all along.

The rain pounded harder, and everything inside me surged toward him—reckless, hungry, breaking every rule I'd set for myself.

"Want another drink?" I asked, even though he had barely touched the first.

His eyes held mine, steady and full of things we weren't saying. "Sure."

He got up before I could move, covering the distance to the mini fridge in a few long strides that reminded me just how much space he took up and how little room I had left to pretend this was anything but inevitable.

He handed me another bottle without a word and sat back down closer this time. My pulse kicked hard against my ribs.

TANNER

God, she was beautiful.

Not in a way that was easy or delicate. She was all sharp angles and inked lines. Edges that looked like they should've been hard but weren't.

The rain pounded the windows, louder now, like it needed us to hear it over anything else. But I didn't care what was happening outside the shop—I only cared about what was happening inside it.

She was so close I could feel the heat coming off her skin. I was so drawn in I wasn't trying to stop it.

"I don't usually do this," she said again as if she needed me to know what kind of risk she was taking.

I took a long pull from my beer, then set it on the table without breaking her gaze. "Neither do I."

And then I kissed her.

Leaned in slow enough for her to back off if she wanted—but God, she didn't—and kissed her with everything I hadn't let myself feel until now.

She tasted like beer and something sweet and dangerous. Like everything I'd been trying to keep at arm's length since I walked into this place. Her lips were soft, tentative at first—like she couldn't believe we were doing this—but then they parted, and there was nothing tentative about it anymore.

Her hands found their way to my hair, pulling me closer, and that was it. I was gone.

This was reckless. Stupid.

Perfect.

We broke apart just long enough for her to breathe, "You're sure about this?"

I didn't hesitate. "No." Then kissed her again, deeper this time. "Yeah."

She pulled back, laughing a little against my mouth. Low and throaty, a sound I wanted to hear again and again.

"We're in so much trouble," she whispered.

"Good," I said, echoing her from earlier.

And damn if I didn't want to find out just how deep we could get.

It was addictive, the way she leaned into me. The way she took what she wanted without hesitation. The way it felt like we were going up in flames and neither of us cared how this burned. Before I knew what was happening, I had her underneath me on that old leather couch, the weight of my body pressing down on hers, and nothing but a whisper between our mouths. This was insane. Reckless. Everything I shouldn't want. But Jesus, I did. And from the way she wrapped her legs around me, pulling me closer until there was no space left between us, she wanted it too.

I kissed her neck, her shoulder, the line of ink that ran up her collarbone. She arched against me, fingers digging into my back like she needed to hold on or get swept under.

"Lola," I said, voice rough. "We—"

She cut me off with another kiss.

"Don't think," she whispered against my mouth. "Not right now."

Her hands slipped under the hem of my shirt, and I almost lost it. It felt good.

She pulled the shirt over my head in one quick motion, and everything else went with it.

The need for distance, for control. For anything but her.

The feel of her skin against mine was all heat and madness. Then she kissed me again. Harder. Deeper. Like we'd both been starving for this and finally got brave enough to admit it.

Her touch moved over me—fingers tracing muscle, scar, everything I thought I'd have to protect—and didn't flinch from any of it. The raw honesty in the way she took me in almost gutted me. It didn't matter we were on an old leather couch with rain hammering down around us—it felt like the only place I wanted to be.

I shifted, rolling her on top of me, loving the weight of her body pressing down on mine. She paused a second, propped up on one arm, eyes searching my face like she needed to be sure this was happening.

"You're different," she said quietly.

And before I could answer—before I could tell her how she made me feel more alive than I had since that day in the desert—she pulled her tank top over her head.

And God, if the sight of her didn't make my heart stop. Ink and skin, all fire and vulnerability. I pulled her down to me, kissing her like I'd die if I didn't.

Chapter Eight

LOLA

I'd forgotten how this felt. Not just the physical—his weight, his heat—but everything else. The way desire tangled with fear and excitement until you couldn't tell them apart. Recklessness. Want. All those things I'd built walls around and pretended didn't matter. Tanner's hands moved over me like he needed to memorize every inch of skin he touched. His scars pressed against mine made me forget which were his and which were inked into me by something other than an artist's needle. We were making out like teenagers on my studio couch, rain pounding at the windows like a wild percussion line, and I didn't want any of it to stop.

I kissed my way down, slow and deliberate. Felt him shudder underneath me when I reached the waistband of his jeans. God, I hadn't done this in years— hadn't wanted someone like this—and how much I needed him was heady and terrifying. How much it felt like I'd never stop needing him if I let this happen.

He was watching me with an intensity that burned away everything else. Watching like he couldn't believe I was really doing this.

I opened his fly and felt the tension in him coil so tight it almost unraveled me. Then he was free, hard, and ready, and my pulse was racing so fast I could feel it pulse in my neck.

"Lola," he said, a warning, a plea.

But I didn't stop. I took my time kissing up his cock before taking him into my mouth fully and letting myself taste just how much he wanted this.

I lowered my head and took him in inch by inch. My name became a groan on his lips. It made me bolder. Made me reckless. Made me want to give him everything he hadn't let himself feel until now.

"Jesus," he whispered, voice raw and unsteady.

And then he stopped talking altogether.

I took him deeper again, moving with a rhythm that matched the storm outside—steady and wild. His hips bucked once, sharp against me. He didn't have to say how close he was—I could feel how every muscle in his body strained for something more.

And God help me, when he let go, it was better than anything I'd imagined.

It took a while for his breathing to steady. For the tension and heat to unwind into something that felt like relief. I lay on top of him, tracing the line of ink that ran up his shoulder, feeling the aftermath ripple through him. Felt him catch my hand and pull it to his mouth, kissing the inside of my wrist like he needed to make sure I was still real. Still there. Like he didn't know I was already so far gone for him, I'd never find my way back. "Tanner," I said softly, unsure what would come out after his name but needing to say it anyway.

He rolled me onto my back with the kind of care that made everything inside me twist tight again, then kissed me so slow and deep it almost wasn't a kiss anymore. Almost something else. Something dangerous and terrifying in all the ways I hadn't let anything be since—

Don't think, Lola.

But even my voice couldn't drown out the thought that maybe this time would be different.

Maybe this time, the risk would be worth it.

"Beautiful," he said, voice rough and honest.

He undid the button of my jeans, tugged them off in one swift motion, and growled when he saw how wet I was.

The first stroke of his tongue sent a shockwave through me—hot, electric, obliterating every other sensation until all I could do was dig my fingers into his hair.

"Tanner," I said, breathless. Desperate. "Oh God."

The way he took me apart was all skill and chaos. He kissed like he meant it—like he wasn't afraid of what would happen if we burned out too fast or fell too far.

The first wave hit me hard—sharp, unstoppable—as he pressed two fingers inside. He didn't slow down, didn't back off. Just kept going until I was arching against his mouth, gasping his name like it was the only thing left to say. My body arched and shuddered around him, pleasure spinning almost out of control until he brought it crashing perfectly down.

"Jesus," I breathed. "I—"

Before I could finish, he brought his lips back to mine and kissed me through the aftershocks until it felt like I was still coming. Like every nerve ending in my body had gotten lost and didn't want to find its way back.

He pulled away just enough so I could see the fire in his eyes. The heat and purpose and need that could've scared the hell out of me if it hadn't felt so damn good.

We stayed like that for a while, hearts pounding in a rhythm neither of us tried to fight.

I moved first, kissing his shoulder—soft, quick, easy—like I could convince myself this was casual. He pulled me closer until I wasn't sure where he ended, and I began.

"So much trouble," I whispered again.

He shifted so we were face to face, our bodies lined up with nothing between them but heat and a million uncertainties.

"Good," he said softly, like it was the only answer that fit.

TANNER

I shifted, pulling her into my lap. The weight of her on top of me felt like the first easy breath I'd taken in years. I didn't want to let go. Didn't want to think about what happened when this storm passed or how much harder it would be to walk away once the rain stopped and we both remembered who we were. Instead, I just pulled her closer.

She smiled at me, a reckless, unguarded thing that squeezed through my chest.

There was something raw and exhilarating about having her like this, looking right at me with all that fire and intensity.

"You're impossible," she said, tilting her head like she couldn't believe this was real.

"Not yet," I said. "But give me time."

She laughed, low and throaty, and it did something wild to me. Made me want more.

She moved against me, her bare skin slick with sweat, and the noise in my head went silent. Like everything I carried had been set down for a moment. Like I could finally breathe.

I kissed her again—slow, deep, unhurried—and let my hands drift to the curve of her back. She was beautiful above me, hair wild and eyes dark with want.

"I don't usually do this," she said again, but this time it was breathless. Hungry.

"Neither do I," I echoed against her mouth.

"Got anything?" she asked, voice low and edged with need.

I nodded, breathless. "Yeah. Hang on."

The last time I'd been with someone... hell, it was long enough that I couldn't remember—but I wasn't unprepared. I reached for my jeans, found my wallet, and pulled out the foil packet.

She watched me unwrap it, eyes hot and intent on every move I made. I rolled it on with hands that didn't feel like mine, too eager, too unsteady.

She didn't wait—just shifted over me, sliding down in one slick motion that almost undid me before we even started.

"Fuck," I groaned, every muscle tightening as I watched her take me in.

I caught her hips and thrust up hard, and her cry matched mine in a way that undid me completely.

God. I wrapped an arm around her back and held her steady as she moved against me—easy at first, then faster—fingernails dragging down my shoulder and leaving marks that felt better than anything I'd ever known.

"Lola," I said, rough. Desperate.

Her name was the only thing I could manage.

The only thing I wanted to say. She rode me harder, head thrown back like she didn't care if she broke us both. Her breath came fast and shallow, matching mine.

With every thrust, with every movement of her body, I felt myself getting closer to the edge. She was wild above me, untamed and unrestrained, and it was the most beautiful thing I'd ever seen.

I wasn't going to last.

Neither was she.

She reached between us and touched herself in a way that almost finished me right there. "Close," she said, voice tight and wild and everything I needed to hear. Her fingers moved faster, and I was right there with her.

And when we crashed over the edge together, it was chaos. She shattered around me, pulsing and clenching and saying my name like a damn prayer. I exploded into white heat and perfect oblivion, her name a hoarse shout as everything shattered around us. Perfect and brutal and everything I needed it to be.

I didn't know how long we stayed like that—the storm pounding outside, our bodies tangled and slick with sweat and desire. Long enough for my heart to stop racing. For hers to slow against my chest.

Long enough for me to wish this moment would never end.

I hadn't meant for this.

But damn if it wasn't perfect.

I held her there, arms tight around her back, wondering how the hell I ended up on a couch with a woman who was supposed to be nothing but ink. Supposed to be safe. Instead, she was everything.

I didn't want to think about leaving.

"Lola," I started, but she shifted and cut me off with a kiss.

"Don't say it."

I laughed against her mouth, feeling lighter than I had in years. "You don't even know what I was going to say."

She pulled back just enough to see my face, hair falling wild over her eyes. "Doesn't matter." There was something vulnerable in how she looked at me—unguarded and terrifying in all the best ways.

The storm outside rumbled like it agreed with us.

"Then what can I say?" I asked.

She smiled that bare, reckless smile again. "Say you'll stay."

For a second, I couldn't speak. Couldn't breathe. Then, all I could do was pull her closer and let myself believe this wouldn't end.

"Yeah," I said like it was a promise neither of us knew how to keep. "I'll stay."

We lay there in the quiet, skin slick and bodies tangled until my pulse stopped racing and the rain slowed. Until I forgot what it felt like to be anywhere but this old leather couch, with her breathing soft and even in my arms. Until I wasn't scared to fall asleep and wake up remembering nothing but how she fit against me.

Chapter Nine

LOLA

For a second—just one—I thought it might really be that easy.

That he'd stay, and I'd let him.

But then I woke up alone.

I don't know how long I lay there, staring at the ceiling and telling myself this was what I wanted. That Tanner had done precisely what I needed him to do—give me a night where nothing existed but us. No rules. No pasts. No promises we couldn't keep. Maybe I'd been stupid enough to hope for more, but even I wasn't reckless enough to admit it out loud.

I pulled on my clothes and padded barefoot across the studio in the dim morning light, trying not to notice how empty it felt—how empty I felt.

Somewhere in the universe, irony was laughing its ass off at me. Tanner was on his way out of Briar Hill before dawn, before anything could catch up with him, tie him down, or make him feel like he should stay. And God help me, I understood. I understood precisely why he left—and why I wanted him to return anyway.

I put on coffee and tried to snap myself out of it. Heat, caffeine, and a shower hot enough to scald—minimum requirements for convincing myself I didn't care. That this was fine. That Tanner hadn't snuck under my skin so fast that I didn't even feel the ink dry before he ghosted.

More irony: I trusted him enough to think he'd actually stick.

The coffee sat cold in my mug, untouched.

"Don't be stupid," I muttered again, but it sounded more desperate than defiant.

I was still staring into it, trying to remember how people functioned after having their breath knocked out when my phone rang. Veronica.

I should've let it go to voicemail. I didn't.

"Hello?"

"You sound like shit."

"Good morning to you, too, Vee. Everything okay?"

"You tell me," she said. "Pretty sure I heard your heart breaking across town."

I sighed, leaning back against the counter. "Barely after eight, and you're already a pain in my ass?"

"Gifted, aren't I? So will you tell me what happened, or will I have to call in the reinforcements?"

"It was nothing," I said, trying to sound like it was true.

Her tone shifted, curiosity edged with concern. "You sound weird, Lo."

"I'm fine," I said, forcing my voice into something less brittle. More me. "Just tired."

"You're lying to me," she said, but her voice gentled slightly. "Is it bad?"

"It was amazing," I said finally, owning it. "And over."

She paused. Like that was a twist she hadn't seen coming.

"You serious?"

"He left before sunrise."

She cursed under her breath. Not at me—at him. Then she shifted gears so fast I had to catch up. "How do you feel about a burlesque brunch?"

I blinked. "What?"

"Vivian's got a noon matinee today," she said, tone brisk and unapologetic. "Mimosas, lingerie, and family therapy by way of interpretive dance."

"I don't think—"

"Exactly," Veronica cut in. "You're not thinking. You're wallowing. Be there by eleven."

Then she hung up.

God help me, she was right.

I hung up and turned around.

And there he was.

Tanner. Standing in the doorway with a tray of coffee and donuts, hair damp and shirt sticking where the rain caught him. His eyes met mine with that familiar intensity—cautious, careful like he didn't know if I'd let him stay.

I stared at him, heart pounding too loud in my ears to hear anything else.

"You left," I said, barely a whisper.

"I didn't." He held up the coffee, sheepish. "Just went to get breakfast."

"But you—"

"I left a note," he said. "Didn't you see it?"

The breath rushed out of me in one shaky exhale. I hadn't seen it. Just like I hadn't seen this coming—him standing here looking like he meant it when he said, "I'll stay." He took a step closer, then stopped. "Am I pushing too hard, Lola? Because I can back off."

I shook my head, still trying to catch up with everything crashing through me. Relief. Confusion. Hope.

"No," I said finally. "You're not."

Something shifted in his eyes—the same thing that almost killed me yesterday when he'd looked at me like I was all the answers he didn't know he wanted. I crossed the room, closing the distance between us before I could think myself out of it. Then I was kissing him. Kissing him like he hadn't just scared the hell out of me. Like I needed him more than air.

He put the tray down without breaking the kiss and pulled me in with that warm, solid hold that made everything else disappear. It shouldn't have been possible, but it felt even better than yesterday—like waking up to an impossible gift. Like finding out what you didn't dare hope for came true.

He drew back just enough to see my face, then brushed a thumb softly over my cheekbone. "You thought I left."

"Didn't you?" I asked, voice smaller than I wanted it to be.

"No," he said again, firm and honest. "I'm here."

And this time, I let myself believe it.

TANNER

I didn't know if she'd let me back in—didn't know if I'd blown it by leaving her asleep on that old leather couch. But hell, I had to try. The look on her face when she found me standing in the doorway almost gutted me. A mix of shock and relief and something I thought might be hope. Like she hadn't expected to get anything more than a storm, a night, and maybe a little too much honesty to go with it.

I pulled her closer, kissing her with everything I didn't have words for. Everything I couldn't say without feeling like it might get caught sideways in my throat. "I'm here," I said again so she'd know how much I meant it.

I kissed her again, lifting her up and feeling the warmth of her body wrap around me.

She moved with me, easy as breath. Her back hit the wall, and she didn't flinch. She just smiled that reckless smile and pulled me closer, as if this was precisely where she wanted to be. Like I was exactly who she wanted.

"I want you so fucking much," she said against my mouth. It was enough to make me forget why I'd even left. Her legs tightened around my waist, and the heat between us burned away everything else.

I swallowed her moan in another kiss and pushed against her like I needed to get under her skin as much as she'd gotten under mine. Like I'd never get close enough.

Her fingers tangled in my hair. The edge of her teeth caught my lip.

"Lola," I growled, rough and raw.

"Tanner," she said, breathless and demanding. I met her eyes, dark and full of need. "Now," she whispered.

It was a command. It was a plea.

I let her down just long enough for the clothes to disappear between us. Pants, lace, jeans—gone.

She was back in my arms before I could draw another breath. Before I could think about anything but how much I wanted this—wanted her. I rolled a condom into place, feeling reckless and alive.

"Jesus," I said, pushing into her in one hard thrust that almost undid me right there. She held on tight, arching against me, and it was chaos all over again. My whole world narrowed down to the heat of her body and the way she wrapped around me like she'd never let go. Like we'd never have to stop.

Her moans were breathy, desperate things that matched my own. "Tanner," she said again, voice wild with need. Knowing exactly what she wanted, I didn't slow down or hold back. Exactly what I needed to give her. Every thrust was a promise, a confession, a reckless declaration. She started coming before I did, her cries muffled against my neck as she shuddered and clenched around me until I couldn't hold back another second. "Fuck," I groaned as everything hit me at once, perfect and obliterating. We stayed like that, holding on to each other like the rest of the world might pull us apart if we did anything else.

I didn't know how I'd gotten here or how long this would last. All I knew was that for the first time since that day in the desert, I didn't feel like I was running from ghosts or letting them catch up with me.

I felt free.

And the way she smiled at me—the full, unguarded thing—made me think maybe she felt the same way.

"I could get used to this," she said softly.

"Yeah?"

"Yeah."

Her eyes were dark and wild and maybe even hopeful. And for once, mine probably were too.

Epilogue

LOLA

We never did make it to the Velvet Room that day.

Vivian forgave us, eventually.

She made us sweat a little at first—dramatic sighs, long-suffering eye rolls, a "you owe me" tab so long it might outlive us all—but she forgave us.

And now here we were, almost a year later, still standing.

Still us.

Still messy, still complicated, still... more.

I tugged at the hem of my black dress, feeling absurdly overdressed and underprepared as I stared at the gallery's clean, white walls.

Sketches—*my sketches*—were framed and spotlighted like they belonged here.Like *I* belonged here.

A low whistle sounded behind me, and Tanner's hand landed warm and steady at my waist. "You're staring at your art like it's gonna bite you," he murmured against my ear.

"It might," I said, still half in disbelief. "It's just waiting for the right moment."

He chuckled—low and rough and completely unbothered, like always—and pulled me back against his chest.

"You're amazing," he said simply, and it hit harder than any compliment I'd ever been given.

I leaned into him for a second, breathing him in—leather, soap, and something uniquely Tanner—and let myself have the moment.

When I finally pulled back, his hand stayed at my waist, grounding me.

"You know," I said lightly, "this is your fault."

"My fault?"

I tipped my head back to look at him. "You're the one who said maybe I should do something with all those 'doodles' I kept hiding in sketchbooks."

He smiled, and it did dangerous things to my pulse. "Didn't think you'd actually listen."

"Neither did I."

But here we were. Not hiding. Not pretending.

I caught movement from the corner of my eye and turned to see Veronica sweeping into the gallery, looking like she owned the place. Vivian followed a half-step behind, all red lipstick and champagne flair, and Eliza—sweet, steady Eliza—was carrying a giant bouquet that looked like it weighed more than she did.

Tanner chuckled low in his throat. "Incoming."

"Brace for impact," I said, but I couldn't stop smiling.

Veronica was the first to reach us, all smug satisfaction. "Well, well, well. Look who finally decided to believe she's brilliant."

Vivian leaned in, kissing my cheek like I was some kind of conquering hero. "Told you."

Eliza thrust the flowers at me with a bright, beaming smile. "We're so proud of you!"

I stared at them, at all of them—this messy, beautiful family of mine—and felt something shift in my chest. Something *settle*.

Tanner's hand tightened at my waist like he felt it too.

"Speech!" Vivian declared, and Veronica immediately seconded her with an alarming level of enthusiasm.

I shook my head, laughing. "Not a chance."

"Come on," Tanner murmured, teasing. "I'll hold your hand."

He meant it.

And suddenly, standing there with his warm hand in mine and my sisters beaming at me like I'd just pulled off the impossible, I realized something:

Maybe I hadn't been surviving all this time after all. Maybe I'd been building something. Something real. Something that lasted.

I looped my arm through Tanner's, faced the crowd—tiny but fierce—and said, "Thank you."

Simple. True. Enough.

"You're incredible, Lola," he said, voice low and rough with certainty. "I hope you know that."

I swallowed hard, my fingers twisting in the hem of my dress. "I'm starting to."

He leaned in and brushed his mouth over mine in a kiss so soft it felt like a secret.

Someone wolf-whistled behind us—probably Veronica—and Tanner laughed against my lips.

"I'm proud of you," he murmured. "And not just because you're brilliant with ink and paper."

"Yeah?" I whispered.

"Yeah," he said, pulling back just enough so I could see the truth in his eyes. "Because you didn't just show your art tonight. You showed yourself. And you didn't hide."

I blinked hard against the sting at the back of my eyes. "Only because you were stubborn enough to call me out on it."

His smile was slow and sure. "Worth it."

We stood there for a minute—just breathing, just *being*.

And when Tanner dipped his head low and whispered, "You're not getting rid of me now, you know," I smiled so wide my cheeks hurt.

"Good," I whispered back. "Because I keep what's mine."

***

Dear Reader,

Thank you so much for picking up *Ink & Iron*—and for falling for Lola and Tanner right along with me.

This story began with a scar, but at its heart, it's about healing, honesty, and finding connection in the most unexpected places. Lola's sharp edges and Tanner's quiet strength made them one of my favorite pairs to write, and I hope their journey left a mark in the best possible way.

If you laughed, swooned, or maybe got a little teary-eyed along the way, I'd be so grateful if you left a review. It's the best way to help other readers find this story—and it means the world.

The Thorne sisters aren't done just yet. Each one has her own brand of chaos, charm, and complicated love story waiting in the wings. So if you enjoyed your time in Briar Hill, stay close—there's more to come.

With all my love (and ink-stained fingers),

Hana York

***

Ready for More?

If you loved *Ink & Iron*, you won't want to miss the next book in the *Thorne Sisters* series: *Silk & Silence.*

A velvet-wrapped storm. A guarded man who's forgotten how to want anything r eal.When trust is the highest stakes game of all, neither of them plays safe—or slow.

Vivian Thorne built her life on polish, power, and impeccable control. As the owner of the Velvet Room, she knows how to captivate a crowd without ever letting anyone close enough to hurt her. Love is a liability she can't afford—and perfection is the armor she never removes.

Dean Thatcher is a gruff, guarded divorce attorney who's seen every way love can break, bleed, and betray. He doesn't do risks. He doesn't do chaos. And he sure as hell doesn't fall for women who look like trouble wrapped in red lipstick and secrets.

Their connection should have been a brief spark—an impulse easy to ignore.

But the more Dean uncovers the woman beneath the polish, the more he realizes she's the most dangerously real thing he's ever craved.

And the more Vivian lets him in, the more terrified she is that he'll walk away when he sees the cracks no amount of armor can hide.

Walls will fall. Hearts will break open.

And when survival isn't enough anymore, they'll have to risk everything—for a love that strips them bare.

Silk & Silence is a steamy, emotional small-town romance about fierce vulnerability, slow-burn passion, and love without conditions. Perfect for fans of broken heroes, scarred heroines, emotional healing, and off-the-charts chemistry.

Keep reading for a sneak peak of _Silk & Silence_.

Sneak Peak of Silk & Silence

VIVIAN

The mirror never lied.

It just didn't always tell the whole truth.

I leaned closer, smoothing a hand over the silk slip clinging to my hips, nudging a stray strand of hair back into place. The stage lights would be brutal if I wasn't careful—every line, every flaw, every weakness magnified until even the strongest armor started to fray.

And I didn't fray.

Not anymore.

The Velvet Room was my domain—red velvet, old jazz, and just enough glitter to blur the sharp edges. Classy. Controlled. Untouchable.

Just like I had to be.

Because the moment you let the world see the bruises underneath? It took them as permission to leave.

I knew that better than anyone.

Pretty was protection.

Youth was survival.

Love? Love was a liability.

I capped the lipstick with a click, sealing the final layer into place.

The color was perfect.

The smile, even better.

No one in the audience this afternoon would see anything but the woman I built from scratch—the woman who didn't need anyone.

And if, sometimes, my chest tightened a little too sharply?

If there were nights I wondered what it would feel like to be wanted for something more than a flawless curve or a practiced smile?

Well. Some truths you learned to live with.

The knock came at the dressing room door—two short taps.

Showtime.

I stood. Smoothed the silk one last time.

And became the woman the world couldn't break.

The real Vivian Thorne?

She stayed locked away.

Safe.

Untouched.

And very, very alone.

Silk & Silence is available on Amazon.

Hana York Books

Tempting Mr. Dawson
Unraveling Mr. Ashford

***

The Thorne Sisters Series
Ink & Iron
Silk & Silence
Pleasure & Prose
Lessons & Leather

***

For a full list of titles, please visit Hana York's website
www.HanaYork.com

About the Author

Hana York writes fast-paced, heart-pounding contemporary romance packed with irresistible heroes, strong heroines, laugh-out-loud banter, and just the right amount of spice to keep things sizzling. Her books are for readers who love grumpy men falling hard, fierce women who don't need saving, and the kind of chemistry that sparks off the page.

When she's not crafting stories full of love, tension, and toe-curling moments, you'll find her daydreaming about small-town charm, plotting ridiculous meet-cutes, and consuming an unhealthy amount of coffee. She believes in happily-ever-afters, overprotective heroes who don't stand a chance against their heroines, and that every great love story should come with a side of sass.

If you love forced proximity, off-limits attraction, sizzling tension, and romance that makes your heart race, welcome to the world of Hana York!

Follow Hana York for new releases, exclusive content, and behind-the-scenes fun! www.HanaYork.com

Find all her books here: https://www.amazon.com/author/hanayork

Follow her on Instagram: https://www.instagram.com/hanayorkromance/

Follow her on Facebook: https://www.facebook.com/hanayorkromance/

Follow her on Good Reads: https://www.goodreads.com/author/show/54826946.Hana_York

Join her mailing list here: https://www.hanayork.com/subscribe

www.ingramcontent.com/pod-product-compliance
Lightning Source LLC
Chambersburg PA
CBHW051311170626
46809CB00004B/1845